Alfi Beasti, Don't Eat That!

By Kate Hardy

PUFFIN

Alfi Beasti was a fussy eater.
He ate everything he shouldn't
and nothing he should.

"Alfi Beasti,
don't eat that!"

Mum's bags were always tasty…
"Alfi Beasti,
don't eat that…
or that…"

"Or that ...

... or that!"

Grandma's shoes were very tempting too.

Alfi's mum had tried everything...

"Alfi Beasti,
why not try this?
It's tasty and healthy –
I'm sure you'll like fish!"

...but Alfi just wouldn't eat anything he was supposed to.

"Alfi Beasti,
you must eat your dinner.
You're going to get
thinner and thinner."

"Alfi Beasti, it's the
middle of the night;
of course you're hungry,
you didn't eat a bite!"

Then Alfi's mum and dad had an idea...

"We're taking you out for a treat today.
The posh shop in town has a new cafe.
Roasted slugs and porcupine tails,
pickled pigeon and purée of snails ...

soufflé of woodlice
and hot buttered mice ...

... come on, Alfi –
it's going to be nice!"

But Alfi didn't think it
sounded like a treat...

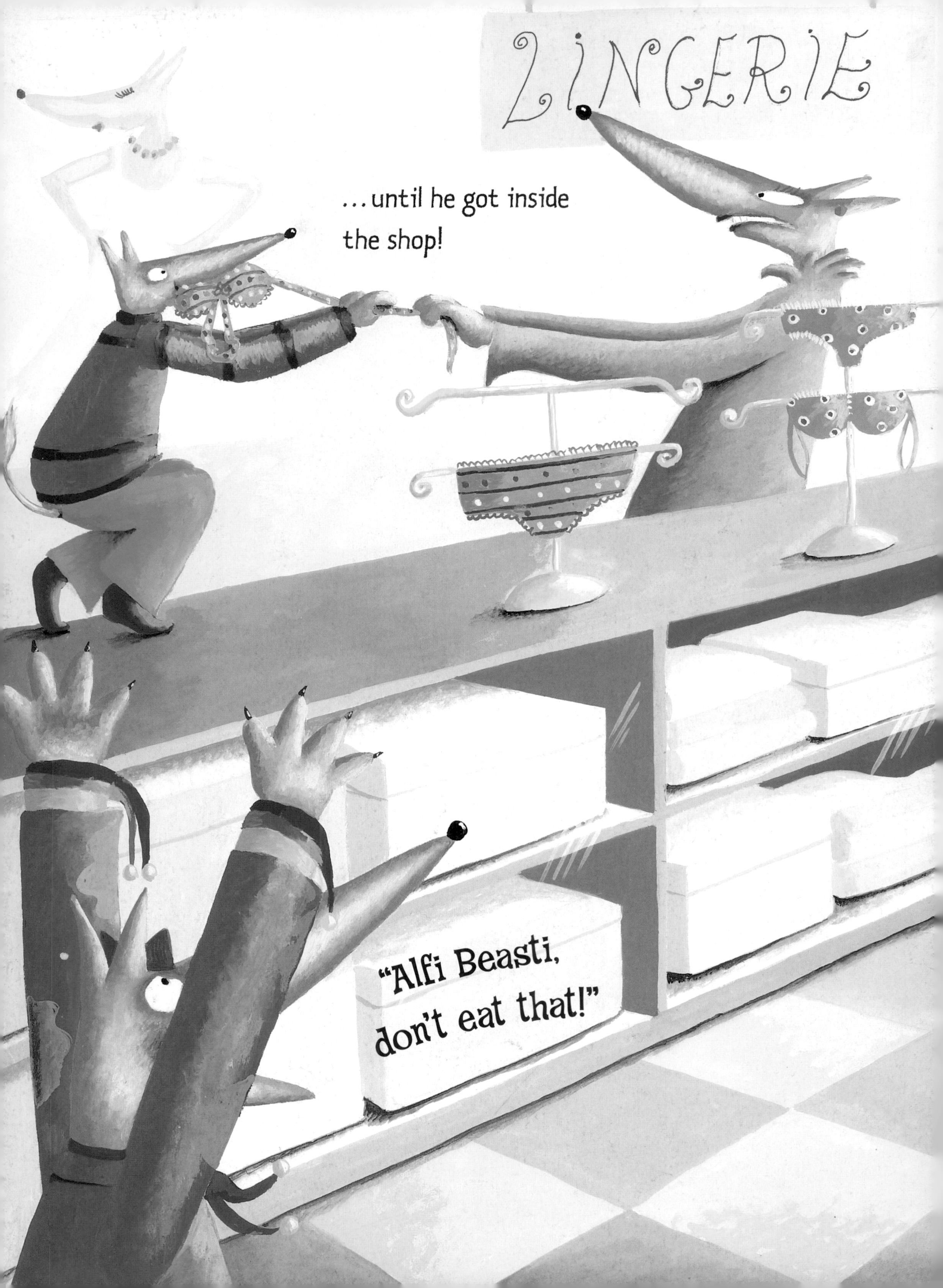

...until he got inside
the shop!

"Alfi Beasti,
don't eat that!"

"And, Alfi, stop!

Not that HUGE, expensive . . .

. . . HAT!"
Softbungelows Restaurant
Tasmanian Termite Soup
with a hint of fresh toad.
or
pickled pigeon paté
Dish of the day
petrified partridge
on a sofa of pink cabbage
Desserts
weasel feet cake
with fresh
cream
or

Lunch was *not* a success.

"Alfi, this has GOT TO STOP!
You were supposed to eat lunch,
not the rest of that shop.
It's your birthday tomorrow; everyone's coming!
If we make a HUGE tea, will you PLEASE eat something?"

That night, Alfi couldn't wait for the next day…

"Alfi Beasti, we can see you peeping.
Go back to bed – you're meant
to be sleeping."

When at last it was Alfi's birthday, everyone was enjoying themselves so much they didn't notice how late it was...

"Look at the time – it's twelve o'clock. The house is a mess and we've still got to shop..."

But Grandma's special presents came to the rescue...

"Don't you worry
about the tea.
We can fix it,
Alfi and me."

So Alfi put on the new chef's outfit Grandma had bought him and they got to work in the kitchen.

"Stirring and mixing,
cooking and baking,
Alfi and Grandma are busily making ...

... Alfi Beasti's birthday FEASTI!
All home-cooked and amazingly tasty!"

"Try some broccoli trees
and banana canoes,
pizza fish and some
toffee gnus ..."

"A spoonful of
wobbly jelly cat and some
incredible, edible birthday
cake HAT!"

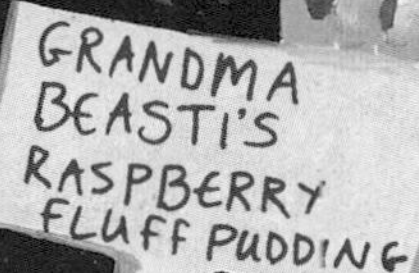

The next day...

"Wow, what a party yesterday!
What a scrumptious yumptious sort of a day!
Alfi Beasti, your cooking was great,
you ate and you ate and you ate and you ATE!
But what about today?"

Well ... if you let
me help with every dish,
and we never again
have that scary fish.
Then ...

". . . Alfi Beasti does eat this!"
Mmm. Not so bad after all!

"Alfi Beasti does eat this ...

and this ...

and this …

and this!”

"I still don't like sprouts, though!"

The End

 For Ezra, the olive-eater 

PUFFIN BOOKS
Published by the Penguin Group: London, New York, Australia, Canada, India, New Zealand and South Africa
Penguin Books Ltd, Registered Offices: 80 Strand, London WC2R 0RL, England

www.penguin.com

First published in 2004
1 3 5 7 9 10 8 6 4 2

Made and printed in China
ISBN 0-670-91301-4 Hardback
ISBN 0-140-56909-X Paperback